Uh-Oh!

by
Shutta Crum

Illustrated by
Patrice Barton

Alfred A. Knopf
New York

"Uh-oh."

"Uh-oh…"

"Uh-oh!"

Awwk!

"Uh-oh."

"Uh-oh."

"Uh-oh."

"Uh-oh!"

"Uh-oh."

"Uh-oh!"

THIS IS A BORZOI BOOK PUBLISHED BY ALFRED A. KNOPF

Text copyright © 2015 by Shutta Crum

Jacket art and interior illustrations copyright © 2015 by Patrice Barton

All rights reserved. Published in the United States by Alfred A. Knopf,

an imprint of Random House Children's Books, a division of Random House LLC,

a Penguin Random House Company, New York.

Knopf, Borzoi Books, and the colophon are registered trademarks of Random House LLC.

Visit us on the Web! randomhouse.com/kids

Educators and librarians, for a variety of teaching tools, visit us at RHTeachersLibrarians.com

Library of Congress Cataloging-in-Publication Data

Crum, Shutta.

Uh-oh! / story by Shutta Crum ; pictures by Patrice Barton.—First edition.

p.   cm.

Summary: Two toddlers have a nearly-silent adventure at the beach.

ISBN 978-0-385-75268-8 (trade) — ISBN 978-0-385-75269-5 (lib. bdg.) —

ISBN 978-0-385-75270-1 (ebook)

[1. Beaches—Fiction. 2. Play—Fiction.] I. Barton, Patrice, illustrator. II. Title.

PZ7.C888288Uh 2015

[E]—dc23   2013041017

The illustrations are pencil sketches colored digitally.

MANUFACTURED IN CHINA

April 2015 10 9 8 7 6 5 4 3 2 1 First Edition

Random House Children's Books supports the First Amendment and celebrates the right to read.